I0549006

15 Dress Adventures
& One Skirt Tale

Shantelle!

Copyright © 2016 Shantelle!

All rights reserved.

ISBN: 0692738932
ISBN-13: 978-0692738931

DEDICATION

I'm dedicating my book to every experience –
the people and places that have been an inspiration
to helping me write each and every magical story.

Thank you!

CONTENTS

ACKNOWLEDGMENTS

Cheers to my best friend, business partner and creative partner in crime. Thank you for being the perfect example of a true friend as we continue to dine out, discuss the latest TV episode of *Silicon Valley* and laugh the day away, amongst brainstorming numerous brilliant business ideas.. it's always a think tank of fun! I appreciate your friendship immensely. Team work continues to make the dream work! Shake & Bake!

Sending tons of love to my family who is always there for me! Thank you for helping celebrate my very first Christmas at my home by the beach by flying into town from the Northwest…meant the world to me. Every phone call & visit brightens my day & rocks my world!

Many thanks to the wordsmith-of-the-south, a dear friend and brilliant editor who gave a helping hand during the editing process as well as making me laugh nonstop on a nearly daily basis. Great minds…you know the rest!

Thank you to my true friends who are like family, may the fun times continue as we have fun making our dreams come true!

A huge thank you to the talented photographer and amazing friend who snapped the image of me for the *about the author* section.

Thank YOU for reading about my many adventures, I am forever grateful and will continue to write more.

Thank you to all of the fashion designers around the world for making so many gorgeous dresses, my walk-in closet is full of dresses that I absolutely love. Thanks for continuing to amaze me.

Thank you so much to all of the people, places and experiences that have led me to write yet another book, my third book, which I'm truly proud of, 15 Dress Adventures & One Skirt Tale! Yay!

INTRO

Have you ever walked into your closet and realized that each article of clothing has a story to tell? Did an exciting moment come to mind? Did you feel the thrill of buying a dress for a special occasion? Did you perhaps have fond memories of travels while you wore a particular item of clothing? Do you remember fun events with family members or friends while wearing a piece of clothing? Recently, I walked into my closet and stood there trying to decide what to wear and immediately started remembering moments I've had while wearing certain clothing, particularly while wearing dresses. I naturally sat right down in my closet and started to write down fun experiences I've had while wearing certain dresses. Since most of my wardrobe consists of dresses, I decided to write a few dress tales. Stories came to mind while wearing long flowing dresses, glamorous gowns or event short and sassy dresses.

The dresses tell stories including elements of surprise, adventures while traveling around the globe, the thrill of meeting someone new, the heartbreak of letting someone go, a girls' night out and I even included one very magical skirt tale; a fairytale! There are family tales, new boy as well as ex boyfriend tales and even stories of being introduced into exclusive worlds that not everyone can obtain a ticket to attend. My dresses spoke volumes to me as I sat in the middle of my closet and looked around, the stories seemed to nearly write themselves.

Next time you walk into your closet, stop for a moment, look around and see what adventures come to mind. Can you think of an event you attended while you were wearing a particular article of clothing, your thoughts while wearing the clothing, someone new you may have met, or maybe even something you may accomplished while wearing a particular piece of clothing? See what comes to mind. After all, each piece has a story waiting to be told; a closet full of tales.

I invite you to flip on the switch and take a walk through my closet as the crystal chandelier illuminates each story, one flowy dress tale at a time. Hold on tight, because my dresses are about to take you on a whirlwind adventure. Let's go!

"He had found his way into a million dollar..."

Top Cat

{ CHAPTER ONE }

My friends, who also happen to be my neighbors, have a beautiful black silky cat. While I'm a huge dog lover, this particular cat had purred it's way into my heart. He wasn't like any other cat. KitCat, the nickname I had given him and he responded to, had high standards. He was very particular. He was from the mean streets and found his way into an animal shelter, amongst other cats. While looking for another pet to rescue, KitCat had stolen the hearts of my friends. He was now living the life that many cats dream about. He had found his way into a million dollar beach home. As you can see, he had been rescued and now living the good life.

KitCat shared a home with his owners as well as two other cats, which looked like twins. He had earned the right to go outdoors whenever he pleased. He was given a collar with a magnet attached, which allowed him to go in and out of the trap door of the house. The other cats were house cats and were not to be trusted outdoors. They were known to once in a while escape and get into all types of trouble. Either they sent you on a wild goose chase, went over to the neighbor's house or hid from you. I wondered if they ever had dreams of being a top cat like KitCat. In any case, KitCat had mannerisms that made you meet his standards. If it was time to eat and you tried to give him leftovers, he refused. Not only did he refuse to eat, he would turn his head away when you placed him in front of his bowl. He would smell the food and look at you as if asking why are you trying to fool me. You actually had to open up a fresh can of cat food in front of him and place in his bowl, so that he could approve and then proceed to eat. KitCat knew his worth and didn't accept anything less than the very best.

KitCat and I became fast friends and we were very fond of each other. We both had experience in the entertainment industry. While I was a print model, he charmed his way into an infomercial and responded on cue. We spent time together as he cuddled up to me as I typed away on my MacBook Pro. He often slept in bed with me and layed right beside me. He even found his way into a photo shoot with me and at times, he responded to me as if he knew what I was saying to him. He seemed like he wanted to go explore the world with me, because often times when I was preparing to travel, he would place himself inside of my luggage on top of my clothes and even on top of closed suitcase. Once, while walking I slipped and fell onto the floor and started to lightly cry and I promise you, I was shocked when the cat started to whine right alongside me, which made me feel better. KitCat was one standout cat, whom I had a special bond with.

One Thanksgiving, I was in my long colorful dress, which looks like a dress an actual doll could wear. I was immediately attracted to the dress while shopping at a friend's boutique and I had to have it. The dress was not the typical dress I would wear. Though it was a long, floor-length dress, it was fitted at the top, but puffed out in a subtle way displaying a beautiful print. It was the kind of dress that you wanted to twirl around in. In the process of eating dinner, I went over to the door where the cats had gathered to look outdoors together. I kneeled down and had little pieces of stringy baked chicken to give them as a treat. Immediately, the two other cats were excited and walked over to me, stepping their little paws all over my dress along the way. KitCat stood back awaiting his turn and to my surprise, refused to step on my dress. He stayed on the floor, away from the dress as I fed him his chicken treats. Wow! As you can see, some cats stand out from the rest and they deserve your attention.

I miss my KitCat. He got sick one day and a vet would stop by the house to give him IV once a week. During the IV treatments, he seemed angry and would whine nearly the entire time. Afterwards, he would want time alone and often walked away and found a hiding place within the house. He came around to hang out with me when he felt better. When I received news that he had passed, after living a long and exciting life, I nearly cried myself to sleep remembering the fun times with the only cat I truly loved thus far. He was one cool cat with standards that reached mine and therefore, we had mutual respect for each other. KitCat had earned his title as one Top Cat.

"...a voice asked us to place on our masks!"

Wedding Masquerade

{ CHAPTER TWO }

One afternoon, I went over to check my mailbox since the mailman had just left. Upon a stack of envelopes, there was an unexpected, medium size box, which peaked my curiosity. I raced back inside to see what was inside of the package. To my surprise there was a beautiful purple box with a scroll inside. I slipped off the gold tassel and unrolled the scroll and I was met with a wedding invite of a friend, how fancy I thought. I immediately sent in my RSVP. What a wedding this would be! After all, the invite had already peaked my curiosity.

I immediately thought back to being home for Christmas just a few months back. While out shopping, I was walking through a store and stumbled upon the most beautiful, sparkly, periwinkle blue lace mermaid dress that stopped me right in my tracks. The dressing room was calling out to me and I immediately tried on the gown. There was only one size, definitely waiting for me. While slipping the dress up over my body, it happened to fit me perfectly, as if tailored to perfection. I stepped out of the dressing room as the dress swayed. I walked down the hall and was met with a mirror that made my heart nearly stop at first glance. The dress was pure princess perfection, it was definitely special. I knew at that very moment that the dress was meant for me to take home, especially after I looked at the price. How is it possible that such a beautiful gown was on sale at such a low price. It looked like a million bucks, definitely worth more than the price had stated. I took the gown to the counter, not sure where I would wear it, but I knew it would be someplace special.

I knew the periwinkle dress was the perfect dress to wear to the wedding. I also went shopping for the perfect silver strappy high heels to wear with the gown. Months later, the wedding day of my friends had arrived and off on an hour road trip my guest and I went. The weather was beautiful and sunny, therefore, I knew it would be a great idea to curl my hair ahead of time and clip my hair up for the drive, so my hair would stay in tact. The music was blaring along the way and the unexpected traffic before us had slowed us down a bit. However, we arrived in time with less than an hour to spare. We were starving and therefore immediately found a place to sit down and get a quick bite nearly right across the street from the venue. After dining, our fortune cookies read:

"Be careful in whom you share your confidence" and "Follow the advice of your heart!"

I found the fortunes to be fitting, since we were heading to a wedding. We parked the car and headed into the venue, a well-known hotel, and into one of the dressing suites we went and got dressed. I felt like a goddess when I slipped on my gown, stepped into my silver strappy heels and my hair cascaded down my back perfectly, seeming happy to be released from the hair clip in all of its tousled glory. We were ready to go. While meeting up with friends before entering the chapel, we took photos when suddenly a bird flew by to welcome me to the event. The bird had pooped on my shoulder! Lucky me! I raced to the women's room and washed myself off with soap and water. I was back in time to walk into the chapel, which was grand in stature.

Upon entrance, I was met with gold immediately before me, including a gold mirror off to the side situated high upon the wall. My friends and I walked down the aisle and sat on the left side of the chapel. Moments later, the bridesmaids and groomsman marched down the aisle. This was already not your everyday wedding. The brides wore black silk dresses along with long silk black gloves and fascinators. As they lined up on both sides in the front of the church, the place went silent with a few audible gasps once the doors opened once again and there stood the gorgeous bride with her dad. We were all captivated at once as they took slow strides down the aisle, as the train of the bride's gown flowed nearly half of the aisle behind her. She looked like a princess as her veil left an aura of mystique. The priest took over the ceremony, also announcing that the happy couple had met online through a very popular matchmaking service, which commercials ads are well known and played on TV on a regular basis. When the ceremony was over, the happy couple walked back down the aisle to go change and get dressed for the reception.

Upon entering the reception hall, which looked unassuming, my friends and I were met with red and purple mood lighting. The place looked incredibly romantic with the lighting alone. Once walked ahead a few feet, a gold three-tiered cake stood before us with gold coins and jewels upon a red silk tablecloth. We couldn't help but get drawn to get a closer look at the cake; the presentation was beautiful. The wedding cake was absolutely gorgeous, elegant and quite clearly looked as it was fit for royalty. As we walked down the grand staircase, which each twist and turn every few steps, we were escorted to our tables.

Upon sitting at table one, where our nameplates directed us, we were met with gorgeous exotic flowers as the centerpiece. We noticed that there was a colorful Mardi Gras type mask, a gold beaded necklace sitting on top of a red napkin and a gold platter. Wow! We were excited to see what was in store. When everyone sat down, moments later, a voice asked us to place on our masks. Very interesting, right?

Immediately, music came on and we were entranced by its Brazilian beats. All of a sudden, we were in awe of quick movements that showcased a sudden blur of colorful feathers and women making their way down the staircase. Once back from shock and awe, we noticed that there were actual Brazilian dancers, which I later learned were flown in from Brazil, dancing their way down the staircase and through the crowd. Around the tables they danced as their sparkly and intensely colorful belly dancer bra tops and tiny hot pants shimmied as their feathered and jeweled headdress took center stage and elevated their presence. The energy of the place was in full party mode as if we were right in the middle of Carnival in Brazil. The moment was exciting as the newly married couple made their entrance amongst the applause. The dancers surrounded the couple dancing as we were all invited to move to the dance floor to join in and dance. What a celebration! We danced the night away and were even invited to a photo session with the dancers. What a fun and memorable experience!

I find that sometimes when you find yourself falling in love with an item, sometimes you just have to go ahead and buy it. Perhaps, purchasing the item may attract an exciting event to find its way into your life. Live life, have fun and most of all, go ahead and buy that dress. You never know where it may take you! Allow adventure into you life!

"I nearly dropped my iPhone when I read ..."

Purple Reign

{ CHAPTER THREE }

It was an early Thursday morning and I was in the process of getting dressed. I had my music blaring from my Kindle Fire HD through my red Beats Pill that my brother had given me one Christmas as a gift. I was listening to the IHeartRadio Fetty Wap station...squaw! While trying to decide on which dress to wear for the day, I had stepped into my walk-in closet, smiled as I looked up at the chandelier. Suddenly my iPhone 6 prompted me that I had a text message. I hurried over to my phone and the text was a message from my best friend and it read that the singer Prince had died. I immediately texted back that I didn't believe it. My friend texted back for me to look up the story and I immediately clicked over to the Twitter app and nearly dropped my iPhone when it read that Prince had indeed died. I was in shock. Prince?! Why? How? And I held onto my heart for a moment, as I was very shaky and jittery while I completed getting dressed.

My mind was racing. I loved Prince. His songs suddenly started to play in my mind. I loved "Little Red Corvette," "When Doves Cry," "Erotic City" and most of all, "Diamonds and Pearls," the version with Rosie Gains. I immediately texted friends and family about the news and they were shocked as well. My brother called me right away. Who knew that Prince had been such a huge part of my life and that his passing would affect me this much? I felt as if I knew him personally and I'm not one who fans out about anyone. In fact, I don't even like the word fan, as it seems to almost suggest worshipping someone. I prefer the word admiring.

My best friend texted me when he had arrived and when I got into his SUV, he was playing a Prince song. I felt that throughout the day, I was a bit lost for words. Still in shock about Prince! I was a bit teary eyed and I couldn't figure out why tears were lightly streaming down my face. When I returned home later that evening, I immediately sat on the sofa, turned on the TV and started watching Purple Rain on Vh1 as well as switching back and forth with BET who had interviews and an audience as they spoke about Prince. My heart felt heavy. The songs throughout the Purple Rain movie resonated with me; I loved the beat of the songs. I loved Prince's style. Prince was different. He wasn't afraid at all to be himself, no matter what anyone said. He seemed 100% true to himself and I've always admired that. However, as I watched in awe, I must admit, I had no idea that Prince wore so many crop tops and or tops that tied in the front, bell bottoms and high heels. He always seemed to dress so sharp with a unique style of his own. I also started to read Twitter posts, which included numerous Prince photos, music as well as video clips and performances, some I had never seen before and others I remembered right away. I was glued to my sofa while the memories of Prince were all around me.

To end the evening I slipped into a purple lavender-scented bubble bath as tunes blared from the Prince Tribute on IHeartRadio and when Diamonds & Pearls came on, I tweeted a thank you to the radio station. In the midst of all of this Prince news, I suddenly had a revelation: the reason I loved Prince so much, not only because he was so unique, but his music brought back memories of my childhood in Indiana. For some reason, I can hardly remember my childhood in Indiana – perhaps I was too young to remember. Yet watching Purple Rain suddenly flooded my mind with fond memories.

I could hardly sleep, waking up at around 4am. I grabbed my pearl ear buds and iPhone 6 & listened to the iHeartRadio Prince Tribute for hours until I finally fell asleep. The next morning I woke up around 7am with tears streaming down my face and I didn't want to pick up my iPhone. I wanted to believe that the whole Prince news was a dream. When I awoke and grabbed my iPhone, I saw that Prince's passing was a reality. I felt a bit somber, but immediately got up, dressed and stepped outside to take a walk on the beach towards the Marina del Rey jetty. During my entire walk, Diamonds and Pearls mainly played in my mind. The lyrics:

There will come a time
When love will blow your mind
And everything you look for you'll find

I love those particular lyrics; they really struck a chord within my heart. After my walk, I felt much better, yet still listened to more Prince songs on iHeartRadio. I'm also not afraid to admit that many times while listening to songs about Prince at home, I would dance throughout my home and even at times play the air guitar! Hahah! His music moves me. I even paused while getting dressed in front of the mirror and another time before getting into the shower, to stop and dance for a moment, now that's an expression of how power and magic of music!

While talking to a long time friend who is a hardcore Michael Jackson fan, she said "its like music is the soundtrack of our lives" and I felt that was a very profound statement, which rang so true. The thoughts of Prince made me remember glimpses of my childhood when I lived in Indiana and made me feel a bit more connected with the place that I was born. Memories of my grandmother's living room where my Prince album was propped up on the table next to the record player flooded my memory as well as details of her home. While watching the SNL Tribute to Prince, more memories flooded my mind. His performance with the Batman symbol behind him, while singing the song, "Electric Chair," immediately made me remember sitting on the steps of my auntie's house, what I wore, including the necklace I was wearing, imagine that. Speaking of the "Electric Chair" song performance, which was my favorite during the show, the way Prince plays that guitar had me hooked. When he bends down while playing the guitar and whips his head around, the visual completely rocked my world. Prince truly seemed to be in his element and I can always appreciate a person who has so much passion that you can actually see and feel it.

While Prince's passing came as a surprise and shock to many, I was excited to be going to a 7:30pm screening of Purple Rain decked out in my long purple dress with ticket in hand, ready to relive a genius at work. I was also excited to see him stroke that guitar as I danced in my seat along with some of the songs that played during the movie. Most of all, I admire Prince, because he helped me recall memories of living in Indiana and that experience in itself is priceless! May Prince continue to wow onto his next destination, which I'm sure will be a standout performance with standing ovations!

"After the pink carpet, I slipped out of my…"

A Tale of
Two Dresses
(In One Night!)

{ CHAPTER FOUR }

The time had come when I finally decided to stop modeling. While I am incredibly grateful for my modeling agencies online and offline, people I've met and fun jobs that I had conquered with modeling in: print, calendars, trading cards, magazines, books, as a spokes model and numerous opportunities to travel within The United States, I felt the time was right. My friends, family members and even my agencies were shocked by my sudden decision. I was still booking modeling jobs on a regular basis. I just felt within my heart that it was time to move on.

As a model, I had shown my entrepreneurial skills when I published a swimsuit calendar featuring eleven of my model friends and myself, of course. I enjoyed the entire process of putting the calendar together, securing a photographer, makeup artists as well as locations. I had suddenly recognized how resourceful I had become and I love the way it felt. Always having incredibly organizational skills: it felt like I was in my element when I was putting my calendar together. Also, while modeling, I suddenly felt the spark to start reading more, even trading books with other models at times. I began to develop a love for reading and later on, after reading 76 books in one year, I started writing. When I looked back on my modeling career, I had realized that creating a website helped me book jobs as well as played a major part in helping me to promote myself as a model. I would always get questions from girls who had dreams of becoming a model and questions about modeling.

I felt as though I needed to get rid of the clutter in order to move on from modeling. I proceeded to look through all of my modeling photos that were stored away in boxes in my closet, as they started to surround me on the floor. There were several great memories along the way. Then I ripped most of the photos to pieces and cut up a few with scissors. I only kept my absolute favorite photos and slid them into my leather bound portfolios as a keepsake. I also kept the coffee table books and other books that I have been showcased in as a model. All was well and I was fully on my way to becoming a full-fledged author and I liked the way it felt.

Eventually, I decided to write an outline of a book to give advice to models as well as to tell my story of how I made my dreams come true of being a full-time model. The book seemed to nearly write itself, because of my joy of writing as well as simultaneously helping someone else fulfill their own dream. In the process of writing the book, *Confessions of an Internet Model: How I Succeeded on the World Wide Web*, I was inspired to create a tank top line. I went to a fabric store, purchased unique faux flowers, ruffles as well as unique fabric patches. I took needle to thread and started to sew each tank top by hand and had created a tank top line! As you can see, my creative juices started to flow.

After the book was written, I had help creating a cover as well as a photo shoot for the cover. I was so proud of my book. This was the first book I had ever written and oh my God, to having written a book in the first place, who knew I had it in me? I decided to have a book release party. Calling on help from friends and family, I was able to take my event from a dream to an actual reality! As I always say, teamwork makes the dream work. I was assisted in securing a location in Hollywood, purchasing a step & repeat, getting pink carpet instead of red carpet, ordering numerous books for my event, as well as creating gift bags for the models in my fashion show, ordering posters for the event, designing bookmarks, asking photographers and paparazzi as well as promoters to help promote the event. I will honestly say that this event was a bit challenging at times to put together, but if you know me, you'll know that I'm an incredibly determined individual. I take incredible action to make my dreams come true. My friends and family members from all over came out in full force to help me, which I'm incredibly grateful for each day. I always say that I have the world's most amazing friends who are not only phenomenal, but are always there for me, especially when it comes to fulfilling my dreams!

Remember the tank tops that I randomly created? I decided to add a fashion show to my book release event. My model friends from my swimsuit calendar I had published earlier, whom I appreciated greatly, agreed to model in my fashion show, imagine that! The book release party started to come together as fliers were made and passed out as well as promoted online. I found the perfect pink sparkly dress to wear to the event that I ended up purchasing, while also eyeing a gorgeous black lace, mermaid style dress at the same time. As a gift for writing a book, a phenomenal friend of mine not only flew into town to attend the event, but also purchased the black lace gown for me to wear as a wardrobe change during my book release party. It still blows my mind that friends and family flew in to attend my event. I swear, life can be really be magical at times, which is one of the reasons why I stay in the attitude of gratitude on the daily.

On the day of my event, friends helped me decorate this enormous venue in Hollywood. While I had faith on my event being fun, could the enormous club really be filled near capacity from my single event? Only time would tell. I was dressed for my event in my pink gown, gift bags ready, models had arrived on time and I was ready to go. I stepped onto the pink carpet with my model friends by my side and was in awe of how many photographers & paparazzi had arrived as the bulbs started to flash! The biggest surprise of all was when my Mom stepped onto the carpet to join me, I was so incredibly happy. She had fooled me this entire time telling me that she may not be able to attend my event, because of other obligations, when in fact, she had already flown into town days ago. If you look at the photos of when I first saw her step onto the carpet and embrace her, my reaction said it all...pure happiness, shock and surprise. I was surprised that my friends and family had been so sneaky.

After the pink carpet, I slipped out of my pink sparkly dress. Before the fashion show, I changed into my magical black lace floor-length mermaid gown that was given to me as a gift. I was surprised to see how quickly the club was filling up. The music was on standby with the DJ, models lined up in the tank tops I created and my fashion show had started as the music started to play. The tank tops had been such a spontaneous idea that I was still in shock that I even made them. The fashion show was fun and I gifted my model friends each with fun gift bags filled with items that included a copy of my book, jewelry, bubble bath and other items to pamper themselves. I was so proud. I decided to take a peek out the front door of the venue, standing behind the guest list holder and was nearly speechless when I saw the amount of people in a huge crowd waiting to get into my event. I swear, this night was even more magical than I could have ever imagined.

I continued to dance the night away with my family and friends who are just like family. Two dresses in one night and a book release party as well as a fashion show...it's amazing what one girl can do in a dress or two! I woke up the next morning wearing my black lace gown...apparently I had a little too much fun and would do it all over again in a heartbeat!

"if meeting up for dinner was a date ..."

Falling For Me

{ CHAPTER FIVE }

After stepping out of the car from an exciting day at the Butterfly Pavilion at the Natural History Museum and high on life, because I absolutely butterflies, I encountered my neighbors standing outside. One neighbor I was long time friends with and the other guy I had never seen before. My friend who happens to be an author introduced me to the new guy. We all talked for a moment and the new neighbor started talking about cooking Indian food and I was immediately intrigued. I mentioned that I had traveled to India and that I loved Indian food. The new neighbor said he would love to invite me over for Indian food; we exchanged numbers.

A few days passed and the new neighbor and I had exchanged texts a few times. He invited me over for dinner and we agreed on a day that would work best for the both of us. I was excited. Although I have a tiny frame, I love to eat, especially exotic food, Thai and Indian food being amongst my favorite.

To prepare for the dinner, I went to the bakery and picked up a red velvet cake as well as a bottle of Moscato. I always arrive with a gift when I'm invited to a party or someone's place, never one to arrive empty-handed. While stepping into the elevator and sliding the door open at the same time, the cake slipped out of my hand and I tried to act quickly, but the cake fell to the floor. There was no way that I was going to take a crumbled up cake to dinner. I picked up the cake, dropped off the bottle of wine at my place and turned right back around and picked up another cake at the bakery.

I eventually slipped into my incredibly colorful floor-length dress and heels and arrived at his place, one floor down, with cake and Moscato in hand. I managed to knock on his door with both items still in tact. After setting the items down, we hugged. Upon stepping into his place, I noticed that it felt quite warm and inviting. I immediately noticed a framed reproduction of the famous painting by the artist Gustav Klimt, The Kiss, hanging on the wall. My eyes were immediately drawn to his stack of books. Great, he reads, we definitely have something besides a love for Indian food and art in common.

The aroma of Indian food filled his entire place and the scent was absolutely intoxicating. He directed me to the dining table and I sat while he placed the Moscato in the freezer to chill. He served me a plate of authentic Indian food that he had been preparing for most of the day. I was excited to dig in. We talked and ate and he seemed like an interesting guy. Our conversation flowed easily and the food was amazing. He was a great chef indeed. Out of the blue, he asked if meeting up for dinner was a date, which took me by surprise. I took a moment to answer.

Before I had a chance to respond, he suddenly became silent, leaned back and fell against the window and was about to fall out of his chair onto the floor. I was in a state of shock, not knowing what to do. However, I do remember during our dinner conversation that he had surgery on his neck a few months ago. Thank God I was paying attention to what he was saying during dinner. I immediately, grabbed his arm so that he would not slam to the floor. He began to move around in movements that were unknown to me. I tried communicating with him, but he could not speak. I immediately grabbed my phone, while holding his hand at the same time during the whole ordeal and frantically called 911.

I honestly can't remember exactly what I said while I was nearly screaming with fear into the phone with the operator on the other line. While waiting with him on the floor, he suddenly stopped moving and tried to sit up as his eyes got super wide as if he did not know who I was or where he was. I helped him to lie back down and to just relax. I stayed next to him as I held his hand to comfort him until the paramedics arrived. The paramedics arrived quickly and asked him questions, but he appeared to have temporary memory loss. Once, again, thank God I had listened to him during dinner; I could supply the answer of his first and last name, his age as well as his birthday. He seemed completely confused. The tension of the whole event was broken when the paramedic asked my name and it seemed to be the only fact that he had remembered...hilarious!

I offered to ride with him in the ambulance to the hospital, but he stated that he was too embarrassed. I walked back up the stairs and into my penthouse as they rolled him down the hall in the stretcher. I promise you that that the moment I arrived home, I sat in the dark on my red sofa to take in what had just happened, shocked by the entire event. At some point that night, I wrote him a thank you note. Always one to have great manners, I thanked him for cooking me a great dinner. I also told him to let me know how he's doing when he gets back and I slipped the thank you card underneath his door.

The next day, he texted as well as called to let me know that he was ok, thank God. He actually said that I had saved his life, because not only had I stopped him from falling, which could have caused serious harm, because of his past surgery, but also it was perfect timing that I was there to call 911. I was floored. It turns out that he had a seizure during our dinner, which had never happened to him before. He proceeded to make me laugh when he said that the Moscato that was in the freezer had exploded all over his freezer overnight. I was just happy that he was ok. I guess you can say that he totally fell for me! Hahah! And, in case you're wondering, yes, I did give him another opportunity to cook for me and it was just as amazing. However, I was sure to prepare beforehand this time by doing a few stretches in case I needed to lunge across the room and break his fall!

*"...as the knife glides
onto the second layer"*

A Slice of Home

{ CHAPTER SIX }

Imagine a tall, three-layer chocolate cake with chocolate frosting between each fluffy layer peeking through upon each slice. Visualize a mouthwatering cake, sitting upright with complete confidence calling out to you to take a slice. You immediately reach for a cake knife and as you cut down starting from the top layer noticing the fluffiness as the knife glides onto the second layer with ease and now you're down to the third layer, which immediately falls over, because it's such a delicate slice. Your mouth waters as you inhale the scent of chocolate upon chocolate begging you to take a bite. You slide the fluffy piece of chocolate cake onto your plate and immediately pick up a fork and take the first bite. Each bite melts in your mouth. Your senses are floating on cloud nine, which immediately causes you to close your eyes, experiencing a perfect melody of the best piece of chocolate cake you have ever tasted.

My dear friends, I welcome you to my mom's infamous three-layer chocolate cake with chocolate frosting that is sure to delight upon each bite.

My mom's chocolate cake has been dancing into my dreams upon each ticket I purchase to go home for the holidays since my university days. I look forward to my mom's chocolate cake each and every time. She never disappoints. Every single time she asks me what I want her to cook me for the holidays, I always and without a doubt mention the three-layer chocolate cake. I imagine each delicious slice on my flight home. Once I step into my family home, whisking through the door in one of my long flowy dresses as the scent of the chocolate decadence fills the room, I breathe in sheer sweetness. The chocolate aroma immediately lets me know that I'm back at home and automatically brings a smile to my face. I absolutely have to have a bite.

I put down my suitcase, race upstairs near my childhood bedroom, wash my hands and race back downstairs and open the cabinet to grab a plate. Once the plate is in my hand, I unfasten the yellow strap of the Tupperware cake cover and take off the cake cover. My mom has this particular cake stand since I was a little girl and when we lived in Indiana. The cake and I come face to face and I stand there admiring the way the frosting is draped upon each layer. My mouth is now watering and I'm eager to take a bite. I slice a big piece and with each bite, my smile gets bigger. Each and every bite warms my heart, giving me that down home feeling. I'm definitely back at home. Each day afterwards, I have cake for breakfast at times, lunch for sure and without a doubt, after dinner. Thank goodness for my super fast metabolism or else my mom's cake would surely get me in trouble. By the time my flight calls upon me to return back home, the cake is definitely gone, every single delicious piece. Once I get back home, I have withdrawals of my mom's three-layer chocolate on chocolate cake for days on end and it definitely takes a few days for the craving to go away, at least until next time I return home.

I believe what makes my mom's chocolate cake extra special is that I naturally associate the cake with being home and spending time with my mother as well as with my family. Plus, she specifically makes the cake for me, which is special in itself. The best description of my mom's cake feels like a big warm hug wrapped in chocolate. My mom is a phenomenal cook and has many dishes that capture my heart as well as my taste buds. However, my mom's chocolate three-layer cake will always be my first love, it had me at first bite and has the ability to welcome me back home in seconds.

"As they turned,

glowing stars started to
surround Alice and ..."

One Skirt Tale

{ CHAPTER SEVEN }

Alice was in tears. She had just broken up with her boyfriend after attempting to check her email on his laptop, when suddenly a photo of another girl and her boyfriend popped onto the screen and they were clearly not just friends. When she confronted her boyfriend, he denied it all and said they were just friends. Alice knew she had to follow her instincts and on the spot, she broke up with him and took a taxi home.

Alice immediately called up her close girl friends and informed them about the breakup and they agreed to take Alice out to cheer her up. All four girls arrived at Alice's and helped her get dressed for a Girls' Night Out. While Alice was always known to be the strong one, the leader of their crew, she was clearly heartbroken at the moment, her confidence was currently on a slippery slope. Having her friends nearby cheered up Alice & the music was turned up to liven up the night. While Alice normally dresses quite demure, her friends had a bright idea to give her a makeover. Tonight, she traded her flats for high heels, instead of a long flowing dress, which covered up her amazing figure, she slipped into a denim mini skirt, put her arms through a silk polka dot tank top and they lined her eyes with kohl eyeliner, filled her lips with pink lip gloss and off they went.

Once stepping into the local hangout, they danced the night away. While taking a moment out from dancing with her friends, Alice was heading back to their table and immediately locked eyes with the hottest guy she had ever laid eyes on. Suddenly, the room stood still as if they were the only two and the moments passed by in slow motion as Alice sat down and he came over to introduce himself. His British accent sent Alice into a tailspin; she was nearly speechless. He was gorgeous. He had a beautiful brown skin tone, thick jet-black hair, bushy eyebrows, full kissable lips, chocolate brown expressive eyes, was well dressed and he seemed very interested in getting to know more about Alice. When he smiled, he showcased beautiful white teeth and his laugh was incredibly contagious. They exchanged numbers and while he pursued Alice in text messages and phone calls, she finally gave in once she was over her heartbreak and her confidence had returned and agreed to go out on a date with him.

He picked her up at her place on the agreed upon night, calling her once he arrived. He stood outside waiting against his car as she walked from the front door. He opened her car door and told her she looked even more beautiful than he remembered, which in turn made Alice blush. They talked along the way until they arrived to their destination, an exotic restaurant in Hollywood.

She stepped into a world of opulence: once pass the velvet red ropes, cabanas lined their walkway as they were met with a huge fireplace at the end, where they turned into an all white room, which looked quite heavenly. The club looked like a beautiful mansion with plenty of small rooms, which entertained with each glance as they walked by. People were well dressed and all having a great time dancing on the dance floor as the music blasted from the speakers. The cute boy grabbed her hand and they danced the night away.

As the song, "Break Free," by Ariana Grande blasted from the speakers, he grabbed her hands to twirl her around. As they turned, glowing stars started to surround Alice and her date suddenly transforms from a normal guy into a White Rabbit in the process. Alice tries to adjust her eyes, closing both eyes during the turn. The next song finds Alice swaying her hips to the sounds of reggae music dancing alongside a cute boy and as she closed her eyes for a moment, in a trance from the music, she opened her eyes and found herself suddenly floating in a boat along the Caribbean Sea. She felt a cool breeze against her face, saw colorfully dressed people with wide-grinned smiling faces and she noticed that that she was sailing in a glass bottom boat wondering where she was going. There was a Jamaican driver sailing along with her reciting a heartfelt poem, completely in awe of Alice's appearance. He offered to show her around and invited Alice to the best restaurant in town along the Sea and she agreed. She ordered Jamaican jerk chicken and salad while the boy ordered the fresh catch of the day, the most expensive meal on the menu. When the bill arrived, he pushed the amount over to her to pay. She paid her portion and slid the bill back over to him and he slid it back to her as if she was to pay for his portions, so Alice hopped into a boat floating next to her and sailed away.

Suddenly the boat took a turn into an underworld where she adjusted her eyes and saw the White Rabbit swimming ahead of her, whom she could have sworn was calling her name with a British accent. Maybe his voice was distorted, because he was speaking underwater. The driver signals for her to step out of the boat, where she is now in a room with an aquarium surrounding her and a note which read "Sip the soup, the truth shall set you free." She sips the soup and is confident as she walks through the door before her and Alice finds herself stepping into a cable car, which took her high into the sky of Sugarloaf Mountain in Rio de Janeiro, Brazil. Once she stepped out of the cable car, a magic carpet appeared and took her on a ride into the clouds where she arrived at a floating tea party. Everyone was floating on magic carpets as they floated amongst one another while sipping tea in colorful teacups. She was invited over to a table of very well dressed partygoers. While floating along, they asked numerous questions: where she was from, how she arrived at the party, what she did for a living and how much money she made. Alice was a bit shocked by how blunt and nosey they were, which she felt was quite inappropriate and was immediately turned off. They appeared to be a bit snobby. She was at a loss for words, when suddenly a cup of tea appeared before her and Alice noticed that words were magically appearing for her to say with every sip. She spoke suddenly, quickly and confidently that she preferred to be asked what she loved to do for fun and what her hobbies are instead of how much money she made. As her confidence grew, she finally decided to leave the party.

Alice directed her magic carpet to take her into the next room. When she looked up on the screen before her, she noticed the White Rabbit appeared and as she touched the screen to see if he was real, she was pulled into the screen and Alice found herself in a colorful world of blue, red, green, orange and yellow powder all around her in the air, appearing in slow motion. She was in the midst of what looked like a celebration of color in New Delhi, India; she was told the event is called Holi. She was bright eyed and amazed at the painted elephants walking alongside of her, the rhythmic Indian music booming all around her and the excitement in the air. People were dancing and singing and having a great time with colorful powder splashed across their bodies from head to toe as they were throwing colorful powder into the air. She had stepped into a colorful world, which was quite exciting.

Alice was invited into a home of a friendly Indian girl and followed the girl through the winding streets of the small village, passing cows and children waving along the way. Upon arrival at the home, Alice was given a colorful bracelet with a bright yellow gemstone on it and told that it was magical and when she truly believed, she would arrive at her next destination. Alice thanked the girl for such a generous offering and closed her eyes for a moment and touched the bracelet and saw the White Rabbit and when she opened her eyes, she was transported to Venice, Italy, where she finds herself already dressed in a red and gold mask in a long flowing gold dress and at a lively masquerade party where she could not see the faces of the partygoers, because they were all wearing masks. She suddenly finds herself crossing bridges, hearing voices in languages she doesn't understand and surrounded by water all around her, when suddenly her hand is taken by a tall boy with a very beautiful accent who leads her onto a gondola and takes her for a ride, singing along the way. His voice sounded lyrical like an Italian melody, a true Casanova. As he starts to whisper into Alice's ear, a girl appears on the balcony of one of the colorful homes along the canal and elegantly flies over and lands right next to Casanova and starts yelling at him, she appears to be his girlfriend.

Alice quickly grabs onto the dock where she slips down onto a sliding board, which puts her on Takeshita Street, right in the middle of Harajuku, Japan. The streets are filled with an incredible amount of people, so much so that Alice could hardly move. It seems as if it's Halloween, because everyone is dressed up in colorful costumes and their faces are painted. Costumes of cosplay, steam punk, Lolita's and girls in laced up frilly dresses twirling umbrellas of bright colors with ruffles with doll-like painted faces were all around her. Alice suddenly felt dizzy and overwhelmed by the crowd spinning before her very eyes and takes off running through the street and steps onto a nearby train in a state of confusion and wakes up along the ride and steps into the next train car over and finds herself in Bangkok,

Thailand.

The aroma of Thai food fills the air, the streets are busy with fast moving cars and there are souvenirs all around her. Ahead of her, she catches a glimpse of the White Rabbit as he quickly vanishes into a taxi. She steps into one of the many hot pink taxis in front of her and asks the driver to follow his taxi. They're on a high speed chase through the streets of Bangkok, weaving in and out of cars when suddenly the White Rabbit steps out of his taxi and onto a long tail boat and Alice follows. She's lost sight of him as she's floating along quickly becoming distracted with markets and shops alongside of her. The scenery suddenly reminds her of floating along the canals in Venice, Italy. Out of the blue, a woman in a long tail boat floats alongside of Alice and offers her a fresh coconut drink. Because of the extreme heat and clearly thirsty, Alice accepts and takes a few sips, which appears refreshing, but she's suddenly in a daze and when she wakes up, she hears voices speaking Spanish. She is confused yet amused to be sitting in the middle of a Flamenco performance in Madrid, Spain.

The dancers are passionately dancing on stage in front of her as she is front row center and has no idea of how she got there. The a capella music filled the air, the dancers attire was rich with color and the guitar players played a happy melody. The girl next to her suddenly spoke to Alice in English and invited her to have tapas and refreshing drinks with a group of her friends. Alice agreed not only because it sounded fun but also because she had found someone who finally spoke the same language. She was new in town and it would be great to have someone show her around. They arrived at the restaurant when suddenly stood a tall Greek God of a boy who spoke with an Australian accent with expressive almond shaped eyes, incredibly handsome as he stood alongside his guy friend. He had olive skin, jet-black hair, bad boy eyes and he constantly made direct eye contact with Alice as his pretty aqua blue eyes pierced right through her. They all laughed and ate tapas and what appeared to be a magical glass bottle of sangria arrived at their table. The bottle seemed magical as it was decorated with colorful jewels inside of a silver square framed plaque, which was attached to the center of the bottle. As they drank, all of a sudden as if possessed, Alice hit the dance floor holding the hand of the tall Greek boy as they danced the night away and one turn on the dance floor too many, Alice, closed her eyes and turned into a new world. She was now dressed in all white and in the middle of the dance floor on the island of Turks & Caicos.

Alice was dancing with the cutest boy who mentioned that he was from Canada and he spoke French. He spoke of his love for playing the guitar as he danced closely with Alice. His mesmerizing green eyes held her gaze as they danced to the rhythmic music. Their skin became soaking wet, as the humidity in the air was very intense on the island. He invited Alice to take a dip into the ocean, she agreed. They disappeared into their separate rooms and reappeared in the center of the resort as he took her hand and led her into the ocean where other partygoers were already swimming and splashing about, though in the middle of the night. They swam together and he playfully chased her as she tried to swim faster to get away from him when suddenly he caught up to her, held her close and was about to give Alice a sweet kiss on the lips and Alice closed her eyes and when she opened them, she felt the desert breeze of sand whip across her face.

She had landed in a desert in Dubai and was now riding on a camel while on a safari. She closed her eyes and opened them again to see if she was dreaming. She was dressed in a long flowing gown draped in beautiful jewels and wearing a hijab. Her hair was completely covered and her eye make-up was done so beautiful in soft colors as her eyes stood out because they were lined in strong black kohl eyeliner. She felt so pretty with her new look as she galloped along on the camel that gracefully conquered the desert like a pro. Suddenly the sand started to pick up and a sand storm was under way as the camel picked up the pace, Alice saw the White Rabbit ahead of her. She commanded the camel to go faster, when out of the blue, he started to fly and caught up to the White Rabbit. The White Rabbit dismounted the camel and ran into a beautiful building with Alice chasing after him and stepped into a room full of snow where Alice was now shivering because it was extremely cold. How was it that she was in Dubai but suddenly standing in the middle of an indoor skiing resort in the Dubai Mall? She looked down at her clothes and she was now wearing a pink snow bunny outfit with white fuzzy gloves on and now onto the ski lift, which dropped her onto the snow and she began to ski down the slope with the White Rabbit in front of her going as fast as he can. She found herself losing sight of him as she jumped off high into the air from the slope and continued to slide down the icy path and slid into the seat of a horse and carriage.

Alice had suddenly arrived in Vienna, Austria and was galloping along the road while wearing a beautiful emerald ball gown with a yellow ribbon in her hair. She was now sitting next to a tall slender boy with a sweet smile who was telling her how excited he was to accompany her to a ball. They approached the royal white castle with gold accents and the horse and carriage came to a halt. The boy stepped out and held out his hand to help Alice down onto the white carpet. They walked arm in arm as he escorted her into the castle with guards on both sides of the walkway. On every step, the carpet lights up and each step looks like a piano key in different colors to the beat of the song "I'm So Fancy" by Iggy Azalea and Alice breaks out into laughter as they walk in sync.

Alice felt like royalty as she glided down the carpet and into a room with brightly lit chandeliers hanging from the ceiling, tables were full of all types of desserts and couples were dancing all around her, smiles bright, in such royal clothing. Alice was in awe of the ambiance and started to dance with her date as he guided her, when suddenly a rock band approached the stage and the guests let loose while their clothes magically changed with the new music that was now playing and picked up the pace dancing wildly and having a great time. Alice jumped onto stage as her date held his hand to help her up. He joined in with the band and started singing. He was the lead singer and as he sang, his appearance changed. His hair was now spiked with gel; he had on ripped jeans, a torn shirt and silver and black spiked jewelry. He was serenading her on stage and as she danced, her appearance started to change. She now had pink streaks in her hair, glossy pink lip gloss colored her lips, a Rolling Stones crop top draped her, ripped plaid jeans covered her legs and higher than high over the knee boots made her stand tall and a spiked collar was surrounding her neck. She found her appearance to be so much fun and as her date handed her the microphone, she started to belt out lyrics which suddenly seemed to flow from her like magic. As she held a Mariah Carey like high note, she closed her eyes and was prompted to open her eyes as the scent of fresh baked bread filled the air.

Alice was now in Paris, France standing inside of a bakery as the cashier was handing her change, because she had just purchased a box full of colorful macaroons. She turned around and suddenly caught sight of the White Rabbit as she began to walk faster to catch up with him, he jumped onto a boat along the River Seine and she jumped on as well. She lost sight of the White Rabbit when she noticed that he started to fly and she touched her magical bracelet the girl in India had given her and she began to fly and followed the White Rabbit. She arrived at the Eiffel Tower and saw him running up the stairs. She began to run and lost sight of him as there were tons of people going up the stairs. She continued up the winding stairway determined to reach the top. Along the way, she felt a little exhausted from climbing all the steps in high heels, when a group of girls with vibrant clothing saw Alice's struggle and grabbed her arm as they stood on both sides of her and helped her climb the staircase. She was incredibly grateful for these wonderful girls who helped her along the way. Though they did not speak the same language, their kindness spoke volumes. When the girls reached the top of the Eiffel Tower, they took a group photo and Alice reached into her pink shopping bag and handed the girls her box of colorful macaroons as a thank you. They smiled, giggled and thanked her. As Alice looked at the view from the top, she loved the way it felt. Paris was gorgeous and was quite the sight to be seen. As she took out her camera and took an image of the view, she saw that she had somehow photographed the White Rabbit on a street nearby.

Alice took the elevator down the Eiffel Tower to catch up with him when she suddenly saw him run into a bookstore. She found herself walking through the cobblestone streets and into the same bookstore. Alice saw the shelves stacked with books and became distracted because of her love of books. She loved to read. Alice found herself slowing down, walking down each aisle of books as she touched the binding of the books as she walked by with the biggest smile ever. Alice was one girl who absolutely loved books. She would always be transported into a magical place whenever she read. Out of the corner of her eye, she saw the White Rabbit go into a room marked Alice in Wonderland and when she stepped into the room, the lights went low and glow in the dark stars floated around the room. Alice was mesmerized by the magical effect and a magical wand appeared in her hand and when she flicked her wrist, she noticed that she was standing in the Shakespeare & Company bookstore in Paris, France. Books were floating all around her and she had to readjust her eyes, because she could have sworn that she saw a book titled Alice in Wonderland with her full name on the binding. Had she written a book of her adventures?

Alice wiped her eyes and was suddenly looking out of the window. Alice appeared to be sitting in a bubble, to her amazement; she was suddenly taking a ride on The London Eye. She was in awe of the beautiful view. Alice was going around and around and was in awe because the ferris wheel was all lit up, as it was nighttime. When the ride was over, Alice stepped off the ride and onto the pavement, which was a moving sidewalk and as she looked ahead, she noticed that it started snowing. In the distance, Alice saw that she was approaching a massive castle that looked so beautiful as it was draped with snow. Alice was now in Hohenschwangau, Germany. As she got closer, her makeup was suddenly glamorous, her straight hair became long flowing curls, she was wearing a peach floor-length gown and a faux fur sand colored coat and pretty jeweled high heels. When she looked up at the door to the castle, the name Neuschwanstein Castle was written in fancy lettering and the door automatically opened.

When Alice walked through the door, she heard music and a massive applause. She wanted to see what was going on and followed the sound and when she walked into the room filled with her friends and family and a few faces she was not familiar with. She was confused as she looked up at the banner on the front of the stage as the banner displayed the words: Congrats Alice on your first published book, titled Alice In Wonderland. As everyone stood as she walked through the room, they cheered and chanted her name. She was nearly overwhelmed with joy, excitement and surprise. She was now a published author. As she flipped through the pages of the book that was handed to her, she noticed that the adventures she had along the way were now titled. She noticed that each chapter was named after each place she had traveled. Alice had tears in her eyes as they called upon her to make a speech, she wiped her eyes and when she opened her eyes again, things seemed blurry and the room started to spin and she fainted.

Alice woke up dancing in the same club she started out in with the gorgeous guy who had the British accent with her friends now joining them on the dance floor and her friends and family members were there as well. Alice was a bit confused as she looked around the room, she noticed that she was back to reality and at a celebration for her first published book. Was this all a dream? Had what she visualized suddenly materialized? She was called onto the stage to make a speech as she read a few excerpts from her newly published book as an author.

As the party was coming to an end, Alice left the venue holding hands with the guy she had been dancing with, her date, as they walked down the pink carpet, which sparkled with glitter and lit up on every step. He whispered into her ear, asking her if she had enjoyed her adventures. She was confused as he sounded a lot like the White Rabbit during her adventures; perhaps they had similar British accents. He held the door open for her to step into the car, which was a white Rolls-Royce Phantom with the license plate that read RABBIT. As he put the key into the ignition of the car, the car suddenly transformed into a magic carpet as they traveled into the clouds. Alice turned around, flicked her magical writing pen wand and the clouds spelled out the words: *Alice In Wonderland: The Around the World Edition.* As the pages flipped through Alice's first published book, the dedication was to all of the readers: Always Believe In Yourself! Dreams Come True When You Believe With All Of Your Heart And Soul! Now go create an adventure of your very own and make your own dreams come true!

"I slowly put one foot on the carpet and..."

My First Time

{ CHAPTER EIGHT }

In the midst of starting my career as a model, I became my own agent. My best friend helped me create a website and eventually, because I like to learn things for myself, I took notes and took over building and updating my website. I noticed that models were getting plenty of exposure online and attending red carpet events after appearing as models on these super popular trading cards.

I thought I would give it a try and asked a model friend of mine who was already modeling for this company for advice. She immediately said that I had to have an agent to even submit my photos and resume. I thanked her, thought about it for a cool second and decided to be my own agent and give it a try. I looked through my model accomplishments thus far and compiled a resume. Yes, it may surprise you that even as a model, a resume may be required at times. I also attached my model card with numerous photos of myself displaying my range of looks as a model. I also decided to write a note to the trading card company introducing myself, like a cover letter.

After a few weeks, imagine my surprise when the trading card company contacted me via email. They wanted to schedule a photo shoot with me to be photographed by their trading card photographer. I was so excited. They also gave me the amount that I would be paid and because I booked the job myself, guess who got paid the full amount including the percentage the agent would normally get? Oh yes. ME! It really does make a difference when you take initiative and go after your dreams full force, no matter what anyone says.

The photo shoot went smoothly. My makeup was fabulous, I was done up as a glamour girl. I had never had my makeup done like this before and I was excited by the results. The photographer was easy to work with as I modeled different outfits. I was super excited weeks later when I saw the results of the photo shoot and now had the trading cards in my hand. Okay, maybe overjoyed was more like it. I was then invited to my very first red carpet event as a model. I was both excited and nervous at the same time. It's wild when you accomplish something that was once just a dream and suddenly it becomes a reality. It's what I wanted, right?

I had to select the perfect outfit to attend my first red carpet event. Okay, to be honest, this would be my very first red carpet event, solo. I had once been invited to a red carpet, very glamorous movie premiere by a celebrity. My image standing next to him ended up being in a tabloid and I was described as "dreamy." I was shocked out of my mind that they even included me in the photo at all. I was flattered and said not a word when paparazzi asked me my name and questions that night. After all, it was his night, not my night. I ended up having a blast at the premiere and was grateful for attending such a glamorous event for the first time. I might add that this was also my very first time ever riding in a limo.

Since that story is now out of the way, I can go onto my very own solo red carpet experience. I went through my wardrobe and tried on tons of outfit combinations.

Clothes were everywhere. As you may know, I absolutely love to wear long flowing dresses, but this time I wanted to wear something different. The weather was beautiful outside and it would be quite warm outside, so can you believe that I actually decided to wear a mini dress?

I did my own makeup and curled my hair. I wore a coral mini dress and stepped into my heels and I was ready to go. My friends and I went to the event together. I was so excited to make my debut on the red carpet. Yet, I noticed on the drive to the event that I was a bit frightened at the same time. I tried to keep my cool around my friends along the way as to show no fear. As we slowly approached the event in Hollywood as if in slow motion, the venue was lit up with bright lights and there were plenty of people standing outside. My heart started to beat overtime. I was full on afraid to get out of the car. My friends and I started to walk up to the venue and I decided to skip the red carpet. My friends were in shock. They were proud of me that I would be walking the red carpet for the first time and excited that I was now on the trading cards. My nerves had gotten the best of me from head to toe as I began to tremble a bit. What if I stepped onto the carpet and none of the photographers or paparazzi even noticed? What if I tripped down the red carpet? What if the person with the guest list didn't even have my name listed?

My friends made me stop for a moment to breathe, while encouraging me that I would be just fine. I was nervous, because I was not allowed to have a guest with me as I walked down the carpet. I would have to walk down the red carpet all by myself, which terrified me. My friends assured me that they would cheer me on even if the photographers did not take a photo and to just go do it. They also told me that they would be there waiting for me when I stepped off the red carpet, ready to go have fun at the party and celebrate my trading card debut. With a bit of reluctance, I slowly walked over to the woman holding the guest list, shaking lightly, as I parted ways from my friends, terrified as ever. She asked my first and last name. She was surprisingly incredibly friendly. Someone wrote my name with a marker on what looked like a miniature dry erase board. The friendly woman instructed me to proceed onto the carpet after I was introduced to the photographers & paparazzi. After the gentleman stepped onto the red carpet, he held up the board with my name on it. I slowly put one foot on the carpet and to my surprise, the photographers and paparazzi started to call my name. I suddenly was no longer as tense and afraid as before. They helped me along the way, instructing me which way to turn and calling my name to look their way. As I continued down the red carpet stopping to pose left and right, I noticed that I felt absolutely relaxed, my posture was confident, my nervous smile was now natural and I had done it. I had walked down my first Hollywood red carpet and I had survived after all.

Sometimes, what appears as a scary moment is just made up in your mind, fear of the unknown. You have to get out of your head, get out there and just do it, you will eventually relax and most all, you will survive. As I stepped off the red carpet, I felt so proud of myself. My friends were also right there cheering me on and now taking me inside the venue to go celebrate. With each red carpet after that, I became more relaxed and the experience felt a bit more natural. As Susan Jeffers says, *Feel The Fear... and Do It Anyway*! And so I did and the experience felt amazing!

"in complete shock when they were told..."

A Very Veggie Christmas

{ CHAPTER NINE }

I was excited and feeling on top of the world. My mom had just told me that eight of my family members would be flying over from the northwest to LAX; Venice Beach, CA to spend Christmas with me. I had recently moved to my dream destination by the beach earlier this year; this would be my first official Christmas celebrated at the beach with my family joining me. My family was also excited to be spending Christmas in warmer weather as well. Christmas 2016 was going to be the best ever. We had plenty of plans of going to amusement parks, hanging out at the beach, dining out and whatever else they had in mind. I was thrilled.

My family arrived at LAX and took a while to get my place; traveling with my niece and nephew under the age of 3 and securing both cars at the rental desk took a bit more time than expected. I had a surprise waiting for them. I have a number of friends who happen to be amazing chefs and one in particular who once had a catering business had graciously prepared a meal to welcome my family. She prepared string beans, seasoned baked chicken, rice and peas as well as dessert. Once my family arrived, I was excited to see everyone and while they were also thrilled to see me, they were even more surprised to see the food sprawled out on the table.

Believe it or not, the weather had taken a turn for the worse. In all of the years that I've lived in California, this was by far the coldest weather I had experienced thus far. Everyone was also surprised by the incredibly chilly weather. My mom and I wanted to have a moment to ourselves; we booked an appointment at the nail salon, walked right over and both got manicures and pedicures, which was fun. Afterwards, we tried walking on the pier, but the wind was so fierce and the sand was airborne all around us, so we had to hurry back indoors. The weather was a complete mess. The visual of taking walks on the beach while the sunshine was shining bright and hanging out on beach towels in bikinis and swim trunks enjoying the usually tropical-like weather was suddenly a fantasy.

My nephew suddenly became under the weather rather quickly, having just recently had a flu shot, which was surprising. He became sick and had to be rushed to urgent care after having a temperature of 103. Disneyland was cancelled. A trip to visit Universal Studios was cancelled. My perfect Christmas was suddenly hitting me with a strange reality. However, how cool was it that in moments that my nephew felt better, we took awesome selfies and made silly faces and laughed the day away. He even requested that I go into his room and feed him chicken noodle soup with him, priceless moments that I cherished. On our first breakfast at an oceanfront restaurant I couldn't wait to take my family to, not only did my nephew sneeze and cough nearly the entire time, but my niece also became under the weather. However, we still managed to take the group photo, which somehow looked livelier than most of the group actually felt. I was grateful that my family was in town and nothing was going to stop me from having a great time. After all, time with family is the purpose of Christmas anyway.

My family and I had several delicious meals together, some were home-cooked, which meant the most to me. I missed my mom's home-cooked meals from living at home or whenever I would go home for the holidays. However, this Christmas my friend who happens to be a vegan and vegetarian international comfort food chef was preparing a delicious meal for the holiday party I had put together. Guests would include my family in town as well as my friends who are like family. Each year, I manage to arrange a holiday extravaganza for my friends who live here in California before some of us head out of town to spend holidays with our families. This year, my friend and his sous chef would be cooking for a party of sixteen. Friends and family members had doubts about the meal only because the entire meal was vegetarian and most are meat eaters. A vegetarian meal seemed not to be enough to satisfy them. After all, a vegetarian meal consisted of fake meat, vegetables and fruit. How delicious could that be?

I was confident of my chef friend's cooking skills, because I had eaten plenty of his meals and knew how flavorful he was able to make each dish. He specialized in international comfort food and flavor was his specialty.
On the day of the party, I slipped into my floral flowy floor-length dress. How was that for a tongue twister? I decorated and placed gifts on the table as we were scheduled to play the white elephant gift exchange game. The scent of the flavorful meals filled the entire place as guests started to arrive. Chef Dahm was doing what he does best, in his element of cooking. Being the tricky girl that I am, I did not tell everyone that all of the food was vegetarian.

When all of the guests arrived, we had dinner. Lively

holiday music played as guests were mingling and enjoying the delicious meal. A few moments into the meal, the chef and I announced that dessert was up next, fresh out of the oven. Guests asked what sort of meat was used, complimented on the intense flavor as well as savory meal and were in complete shock when they were told that the entire meal was vegetarian. Even some of the guests that knew ahead of time that the entire was vegetarian were shocked, because the consistency of the food as well as the flavor seemed just like real meat, imagine that! They were even surprised that they were in fact full after having a plate or two. The night was continued by playing the white elephant gift exchange game, which livened up the night even more with roars of laughter. It was indeed an exciting Christmas party, which I was incredibly grateful for. On this note, wishing you and your family A Very Veggie Christmas and a happy and healthy new year!

Christmas Day: As sick as my nephew was, but feeling a little better on Christmas Day, imagine his surprise when there was a knock on the door and Santa Claus was face to face with my nephew. He couldn't believe that Santa had actually come to visit him. When does that every happen in life? The excitement in his eyes lit up the room. Santa greeted everyone and had a bag full of gifts. Although my family and I had agreed not to exchange gifts, since they're being in town was our gift to each other, I had arranged for Santa to gift everyone with a present, which had their names attached. They were surprised as each name was called.

During the day, my nephew was up and excited to play with his gifts. The night changed as we were dressed and about to head out to dinner. Plans for Christmas were suddenly cancelled when my sweet little nephew was not well enough to go to the restaurant. We called and cancelled the reservations in Beverly Hills. Plan B was in effect. My brother and I were now on a mission. It was super fun driving around to different restaurants with my brother to see if they had meals to go. Most of the restaurants were closed, had incredibly long lines and had too long of a wait list. Now imagine us calling the grocery story to find out that they were to close in less than an hour. We rushed over, picked up ingredients and made it back home. My brother cooked the most delicious salmon and veggie meal as we all sat around the table and had A Very Merry Christmas. While the Christmas holiday did not go as we planned, the best gift I could ever have ever received that Christmas was spending time with my family by the beach.

In case you're wondering about the dinner menu, enjoy these mouthwatering vegan and vegetarian dishes:

Starter:
Salad and Soulistic Spice Rolls

Dinner:
Chicken Penne Pesto Bake
w/broccoli and bell pepper

Jerk Chicken
Citrus BBQ Rib Tips
w/bell peppers and onions

Spicy Sauteed Cabbage
w/coconut and carrots

Soulistic Rice

Cuban Black Beans

Collard Greens

Dessert:
Cinnamon Rolls w/Pear & Brandy Compote

"I was in the process of booking and panicked..."

Song of India

{ CHAPTER TEN }

Upon deciding at the last minute that I wanted to go to India to participate in the celebration of Holi, I realized that most of my documents I needed to travel had expired. While looking at a website that specialized in group travel, I was in the process of booking and panicked when I noticed that I needed to pay to have my documents updated and expedited right away if I wanted to travel within less than a week and a half. I searched online and eventually found an agency that would have my documents to me in time.

I was on cloud nine as I fell asleep. In the morning, my alarm blared and I was excited to beheading to my dream destination, India. With India on my mind and a smile on my face. I woke up, got dressed, and headed to the airport with my documents in hand. I walked into Tom Bradley International terminal and checked in. I only traveled with a carry-on. There was no reason that I was going all the way to India and risk having my bags lost upon arrival. My flight went by quickly with books, sleep as well as movies to occupy my time. I arrived in Germany for a quick layover. I pulled out my phone to call my family to let them know that I had arrived. Unfortunately, my cell was not working. I was shocked, considering that I had called my cell phone provider in advance & signed up for the temporary travel overseas plan. I could not get my phone to work at all; I went up to the Lufthansa Airlines desk and told an attendant what happened and she allowed me to use her phone at the desk. I was on the phone for over 20 minutes. I thanked the woman profusely. I was happy now that my phone was working and on my way to my next flight. The flight went by quickly and the vegetarian plate was delicious, which I had scheduled in advance.

I arrived at the airport and was immediately amazed at the beauty of my surroundings, everything was so modern. I had been told by people as well as read online that I could be met with dire circumstances upon arrival at the airport in India. The airport was incredibly clean and I loved the larger than life elephant statues that I saw. I walked out of the airport and was met with a gentleman holding a sign, which had my name on it along with the name of the tour company in bold lettering. I walked over to him and we walked over to the tour van. I was the only passenger.

As we started to drive down the roads, I noticed beautiful and colorful saris floating by as women walked down the street. I saw buildings that looked like palaces as a well as a few that looked a bit old and weathered but with plenty of character and seemingly filled with stories to be told. I saw phone lines that had numerous lines connected in all directions with a chaotic presence, but somehow managed to work perfectly fine. I was fascinated by the green and yellow tuk-tuks that I once only saw online and now in real life. The streets were filled with other vehicles I had never seen before along with animals just roaming the streets. Everywhere I looked, my eyes were delighted by something new. I was definitely entering a whole new world, which excited me in every direction.

After driving for quite some time, we arrived at my

hotel. I decided to arrive in India a few days earlier than the tour was scheduled to begin, so that I could start to look around on my own, that's the explorer in me taking center stage. I checked into my room, started hanging up my clothes right away as I always do, so that my clothes can breathe from being trapped inside of my suitcase for so long. I was distracted and excited by glancing out of my window at the parade of people, vehicles and animals that progressed down the street. The sight was like no other I had ever seen. Everything and everyone was so colorful that it looked like a celebration was taking place, but it was just everyday life in India, imagine that! What an exciting place!

I took a shower and slipped into my purple long flowing dress. I fastened the clasp to my multi-tiered beaded necklace, put my arms through my grey jacket to be respectful to the Indian culture and stepped into my platform shoes. After getting dressed, I headed down to the lobby to go explore when I ended up meeting a girl with pinkish red hair from Australia. She had also arrived early for the tour and seemed quite feisty and full of energy. She was a journalist and seemed full on ready to explore, so we decided to go explore together. She had on a black hat, white tank top, denim mini skirt and black combat boots, definitely expressing a personal style of her own.

We first decided to take a ride, which I had been dreaming of, inside of an infamous green and yellow tuk-tuk. I noticed right away that the seating was covered with the imitation of an incredibly popular brand that showcases a brown and gold pattern. There were two men in the front seat, one was the driver and the other was a local. The other man asked us where we were from and what we did for a living. I was also immediately asked if knew Obama personally? LOL! After the local guy found out where I was originally from, he started to sing a Michael Jackson song to me and I must admit, he had a great voice. The Australian girl and I started to laugh as he entertained us along the way. We were also told that books were hard to come by in India and the man said that he loved to read. Amongst seeing the goings on of daily life, we ended up at a shop that sells saris and colorful carpet. The saleswoman immediately came over to me, selecting numerous gorgeous saris for me to try on. She wanted to play dress up. Why not? Besides, the fabric was so beautiful and I had wondered what I would look like wearing a sari. It turns out, the saris were glamorous as I stared at myself in front of the mirror after each wardrobe change. While I had no need for a sari, it sure was fun to lay dress up in Delhi and serenaded on our way around town during my first tuk-tuk ride in India.

"...and others were only
costumed in body paint."

Playboy Mansion Debut

{ CHAPTER ELEVEN }

As a model, I was constantly invited to fun events that I had once only dreamed about attending. I also had numerous agencies online that also contacted me about attending events, which I handled on my own via my personal website. One of my online agencies received a casting call requesting models for an upcoming event at the infamous Playboy Mansion. As I continued to read the details of the email, I was instantly attracted to the event, because it was a charity event. If you know me, then you know that I'm all about a legit charity event attached to a great cause. I noticed that to be considered for the event, I had to send my most recent photo to be approved. I thought it was very interesting that as a charity event that was to benefit the girls of the night organization, they would need to see what I looked like first. In any case, I sent my most recent photo.

Days later, I received an email saying that I was approved for the event. Score! Apparently I had made the cut to help raise money at the Playboy Mansion to benefit a worthy cause. You will not believe what happened on the day of the event. I discovered that my boyfriend had been cheating on me, imagine that. I confronted my boyfriend about the photos I had seen of he and another girl who had wanted to be a model. In one photo, she was sitting in his lap and in another; she was kissing him square on the mouth. When I thought back to where I had once seen her before. She was on his social media page repeatedly, a go-go dancer at the club he was promoting at in Hollywood. When I first saw her image, my intuition kicked in. One time I had stepped into his car and there was glitter all over the passenger seat. I asked him about the glitter and he mentioned that he had given one of the go-go dancers a ride home, because she didn't have a ride. How nice of him to offer such assistance to a go-go dancer who had arrived at the club to dance, not knowing that she had a ride home at the end of the night. I doubted him, but I don't like to jump to conclusion without facts. However, I had evidence this time and he denied it all, saying that they were just friends. I broke up with him.

Anyhow, I eventually pulled myself together and searched my closet for a dress to wear to the Playboy Mansion, where the charity event was being held. I had recently gone shopping on Melrose and purchased a black lace and satin dress that I was dying to wear. This particular dress would be perfect for the event. The dress was sexy without being too revealing. It was a black satin dress with lace peek-a-boo accents down the side of the midi-dress. I found the perfect black strappy heels to wear to complete the look.

While I got dressed, with the break-up fresh on my mind, it was a bit of a challenge to put my Maybelline Unstoppable black eyeliner around my eyes, because my eyes were a bit damp. Eventually, I made it work. I knew my eyeliner had my back. I was dressed, hair and makeup done as I slipped into my new dress and high heels and I was ready to go. I arrived at the parking lot at UCLA as instructed and onto the bus I went to the Playboy Mansion for the very first time. I must admit, I was super excited. I had heard so many wild stories about the mansion and often heard people describe what it looked like. However, this time I was able to see the mansion for myself. As the bus rode up the hill to the mansion and the Mansion was now in full in sight, I was eager to explore.

The mansion was larger than life in all of its brick castle-like features. I met up with at least nine other models that were also booked for the event. We found ourselves all wearing black dresses via the instructions from the details of the booking. We were shown around the mansion. There was a huge buffet of food, bars were fully stocked as smiley girls walked around in colorful Playboy bunny costumes and others were costumed in only body paint.

The event was elegant; guests were dressed in formal attire. I also noticed that the ground was cobblestone. I found it interesting that since most girls attending the Playboy Mansion at any point were more than likely to wear high heels, that the ground was made to be a bit difficult to walk on. I noticed a few familiar faces, one particular popular female comedian who was to perform that night for the fundraiser. Our job as models was to mingle throughout the events in pairs to collect money raised for the charity event to be turned in at the end of the night, easy enough. I met a lot of interesting people in between getting phone calls and texts from my ex asking where I was. I delighted him with the response that I was at The Playboy Mansion, a place he had only dreamed of, but never wanted me to attend. Ha! At some point, I just went ahead and turned off my phone completely and enjoyed the night, excited that he would be distressed with what I was doing at the Playboy Mansion and not home moping over our breakup.

It was cool to see the infamous grotto in real life. While I dare not take a dip, there were people hanging out and around the hidden cave-like structure and pool. A few of my model friends and I sat on the stones and absorbed the scene for a moment just for the experience of having been in the grotto. The event ended up raising tons of money for the charity, which made everyone happy. In fact, my luck for the night was that one of the guests won a flat screen TV in a raffle and offered me the TV as a gift. Now that's not something that happens everyday. I was happy that while this was not the typical experience of a Playboy Mansion party, since the event was only held at the location, the charity route was the perfect way for me to attend the mansion for the very first time.

In fact, I ended up attending the mansion a few more times for charity events. I attended the Playboy Mansion for a Hawaiian theme event, another elegant dressy affair. Once, I even met up with an author of a travel book at the mansion. She wrote a book giving tips and advice for girls who wanted to travel solo. After hearing her speak at a book signing in Beverly Hills, it turned out that we were both headed to the Playboy Mansion for a charity event, so we met up. The Playboy Mansion is full of fun surprises and I'm glad my experiences were more my speed as well as for a great cause.

Birthday On the Go

{ CHAPTER TWELVE }

I remember going shopping at The Grove and finding myself on the second floor inside of Nordstrom dressing room trying on a gorgeous colorful floor-length dress. The dress had a mixture of the beautiful colors: blue, purple, silver and white in an elegant tie-dye way. I was enamored by the dress and did not want to take it off. Though I did eventually take off the dress to try on a few more dresses, I found myself putting the dress back on and knew I was smitten by not only how soft it felt, the beautiful braided detail around the low neckline, but just the feeling of how I felt in the dress and how it complemented my chocolate skin tone. I was a goner and I knew I had to have the dress. Before deciding upon buying an item of clothing, I usually have to reason with myself on where I would wear the dress if I did indeed buy it. The dress cost more than I would normally pay for a dress, even though I was a dress lover and owned plenty. While, I could not think of one reason why I just had to buy the dress and where I would wear it, I knew I was not leaving the store without it. I proudly took the dress to the counter and purchased it and felt on top of the world.

Fast forward, months later, the time had come when I would decide on the perfect place to wear the dress, on my birthday, seemed like the perfect time, since I loved the dress so much. I'm sure the dress had been excitedly waiting for a chance to be plucked out of obscurity as it gracefully hung next to many other gorgeous dresses in my walk-in closet. The dress had waited patiently until the moment was perfect to shine and today was the day.

On my birthday, I received numerous calls wishing me a Happy Birthday and others sang Happy Birthday to me, I was so happy and excited. My best guy friend picked me up and treated me to breakfast at a French restaurant, where we had delicious crepes. I had a savory crepe filled with strawberries, bananas & Nutella. After returning home, hours later, my long time friend picked me up and we laughed over my birthday lunch at a soul food restaurant, which we both loved. The food was full of flavor and plentiful. I had plenty of leftovers to take home. By the time evening came around, it was time for my birthday dinner with my boyfriend at the time.

I had been so incredibly exhausted and on the go for most of the day. I also realized that a few friends who normally call and wish me a Happy Birthday had not called, no worries, I was grateful for the ones who had remembered my birthday. I was so exhausted around dinner that I even suggested that we could just stay in and maybe order in for the night. My boyfriend at the time seemed a bit nervous and kept checking his phone and then suggested we go someplace in the neighborhood and recommended a sushi restaurant. I could tell that he really wanted to take me out, so I slipped into my magical dress from Nordstrom and we stepped outdoors and proceeded down the street in the direction of the restaurant.

All of a sudden we started to pass a long black stretch limo and he seemed enamored by it. I simply glanced over and kept walking. He suggested that we walk over and ask who the limo was for and I thought he was out of his mind and I refused. However, the chauffer called out my name and stepped out of the limo and invited me to step into the limo. I was confused. When he opened the door, I immediately started to scream with excitement. Inside of the limo were at least 10 of my friends who were darn near family away from my real family wishing me a Happy Birthday. When does this ever happen in life? I was overjoyed with excitement that I could hardly speak but kept screaming and smiled and became even more excited when my best friend held up tablets with my great friend from South Carolina appeared on the screen and on another screen was my Mom wishing my a Happy Birthday. And remember the friends that had not called me yet for my birthday? Well, there were inside the limo, so sneaky. I had no idea about this celebration. I stepped inside the limo, music was blaring and we popped open the champagne as the driver drove us around to a destination that was unknown to me.

We eventually arrived in front of my favorite Brazilian restaurant and what I assumed would be dinner with my friends and I was on top of the world. I stepped inside and immediately started screaming again when I saw more friends standing around awaiting my arrival and to share in my birthday celebration. As I walked towards my friends saying hello and hugging them, the table in the back suddenly caught my attention. There was the most beautiful three tiered, amazingly decorated birthday cake with a pink castle on top with my name written in frosting on the banner along with bright star sparklers lit on the sides of the cake which shot out. Once again, I started to scream. It turns out that my Mom and best friend had worked together to have the cake made. The immaculate pink, purple and green decorated cake was a gift from my mother. I swear to you, it was beautiful with a Disney Princess on each level of the cake with the black Disney Princess, Princess Tiana being on top. I was also presented with a sparkly glittery rhinestone crown and a pink sash with the words Princess in purple glitter written on top. I was overjoyed and I can honestly say that I have the world's most amazing true friends and family, which I'm immensely grateful for, simply because they were there celebrating with me! In the midst of all of the excitement, my friends had dressed their dog up with a handmade oversized crown necklace with the words Happy Birthday written with colorful magic markers. I grabbed the sweet dog and held him up in the air, so excited!

As we drove back to my place and dropped everyone off at their car, I sat in the back of the limo just excited about life and the amazing people that I have in my life. It truly pays to stay in the attitude of gratitude; life becomes immensely magical! When I stepped out of the car, gathering my gifts including flowers, I took the elevator up to what my friend's called my Dollhouse and I absolutely passed out. Today was a good day, quite the memorable birthday filled the brim with surprises, but most of all, the world's most amazing true friends and family members, lucky me!

"*...in complete slow motion, our heads turned as we...*"

Hollywood
Meets
Bollywood

{ CHAPTER THIRTEEN }

My confidence had taken over. I was in full swing and back to my normal self with the help of my close friends and family, so much that I decided to phone up this incredibly hot guy I had met in Santa Monica some time ago who seemed really nice. Now that I think about it, I had been unhappy that night of meeting this new sweet guy, unhappy in my relationship with my cheating ex, Richard. I had been sulking a bit the night that I met Mr. Tall, Dark, and Handsome, whose name I later learned was Ajit. He made me feel better, because he made me laugh and smile constantly throughout the night. He was incredibly easy to talk to. My girlfriend had been out on the dance floor all night while I sat as on onlooker, being the good girlfriend or something like that, but remember feeling really sad that particular evening, because of something the cheating ex had done.

Ajit and I first saw each other as I was walking across

the dance floor, on my way to the bar. I looked over to the right and in slow motion exchanged glances with one of the finest men I had ever seen in my life, oh my goodness. He was hot. I mean he was completely gorgeous. It was like watching a movie, in complete slow motion, our heads turned as we looked over at each other, our eyes met and it felt as if my heart had stopped. He suddenly smiled and became even more incredibly good-looking.

First off, Ajit had beautiful thick black, shiny, highly styled hair, mesmerizing brown, almond shaped soulful eyes, a killer smile and beautiful bronze skin. He was incredibly dreamy. Ajit was like a beautiful male mannequin come to life. He was dressed so proper in his tailored sports coat, nice crisp button up shirt, dark pressed jeans and nice elegant and shiny loafers. I immediately kept walking. When I returned to my seat, he came over and introduced himself as Ajit and I immediately noticed his very beautiful British accent; I was instantly drawn to him. I became a bit shy, standoffish a bit, and refusing his dance proposals although he had asked numerous times. It was true; I had a boyfriend at the time. However, he did not ask and I did not tell.

We kept the conversation light, although I was completely captivated by his beautiful British accent as he spoke while looking directly into my eyes upon every word. If you know me, then you how much I can always appreciate an exotic looking man; I was full on mesmerized. Hearing his pleasant and articulate voice, while experiencing his gentleman-like behavior sent me into a tailspin. I left that evening knowing that there was definitely an attraction there, but there was nothing I could do about it at the time, because I was stuck in my unhappy relationship with the cheating ex and was on the verge of breaking up with him. I knew within my heart and soul that I deserved better and thoughts of Ajit seemed to help speed up the process.

Well, Mr. Tall, Dark & Handsome is the guy I ended up calling when I regained my confidence from breaking up with the cheating ex and feeling sexier and high on life like never before. He was shocked and surprised to hear my voice, considering that he had been pursuing me for months. He even said, "Is this my Christmas gift, you finally calling?" I giggled like a schoolgirl and excited to hear that he had remembered me so quickly, since we had not once spoken on the phone until today. He was incredibly charming over the phone, as I was captivated by his accent. Eventually during our conversation, he invited me out for drinks and dinner in Hollywood and I happily accepted. This was my first date after having broken up with the cheating ex. I made sure to look super hot and definitely ready for a little bit of trouble, at least that was my mindset at the time.

I was excited and on a high and feeling fabulous, because I was back to my normal self. There was no need to ever fret over a boy who didn't deserve me in the first place. I took a steaming hot shower, using my favorite Victoria's Secret Wild Madagascar Vanilla scented body wash, following up with the scented body moisturizer and body mist. I curled my hair in long beautiful layers, applied my killer unstoppable, black, no smudge eyeliner, Maybelline, that is. I applied a high shine neutral lip-gloss to my lips, curled my lashes with a 24K gold eyelash curler and picked out something super cute to wear. While it was a bit brisk outside, I kept my style casual cute as I slipped into my little black form fitting midi dress, which had one layer of ruffles at the bottom. The neckline of the dress was just enough to tease, my cleavage giving a peek a boo, but not at all too revealing. Then I slipped into my black velvet heels, high heels, of course. I fastened the clasp to my silver large hoop earrings and topped the look off with a form fitting waist-length black button up sweater jacket, which added more style with its cute buttons and I was ready to go.

Ajit called when he arrived downstairs and to my surprise, he was even more handsome and even dreamier than I had remembered from meeting him months ago. Oh my! He was definitely worth the wait and thank goodness I had kept his number from that evening. And thank goodness he had pursued me all this time, because he was fresh on my mind the minute I was single. How funny, he mentioned, "You are even prettier than what I remembered." We embraced in a friendly hug as he held the door open for me as I stepped into his shiny black Mercedes, which seemed to match his style. The car went right along with his sharp and elegant look.

We chatted as we drove along Hollywood Boulevard and I was in awe, captivated by his presence. We had plenty to talk about and found that we had a lot in common. I had never once been out with such a charming man who dressed in such a respectable manner with such a beautiful accent who was so attentive, proper and kind. I liked the way this felt, this was a whole different type of guy that I had never once experienced. He was a true gentleman indeed and I enjoyed our ride.

Upon arrival at our dinner location, the beauty of the place was intoxicating and intriguing. The venue was romantic with colors of royal blue and deep purple throughout. The place was very elegant and breathtaking at once, just like him. There was a very classic, old world Hollywood glamorous style to the venue, absolutely beautiful with its chandeliers gracefully hanging from the ceiling above and winding staircases along with floating candles all over the place. The lighting was just right and so was he.

Our conversation simply flowed and everything seemed right. He was very much a gentleman with good manners and simply a delight to look at as well as interesting to talk to. While I had a drink or two, I was hardly able to eat, because for the very first time, I felt nervous around a guy. I was normally pretty outspoken, but at the moment I was a bit loss for words. It's not only that Ajit was incredibly good looking, but it was the way that he made me feel…a feeling that I had never experienced before, so it sort of threw me for a loop. In any case, he automatically served me, placing a bit of each dish onto my plate. I eventually relaxed a bit and the date was going really well. Then he asked me to his company's holiday event. I thought, this is much too soon. I had just met him. I'm not sure I feel comfortable meeting his friends and co-workers all in the same evening. However, he assured me that it would only be for a little while, so I agreed. Upon entrance, once again, I was face to face with another incredible venue. The Sophie Hotel at the Rose Love Lounge, was beautiful and elegant with deep maroon colors with a very upscale lounge feel, glamorous chandeliers hanging low, which was quite appealing along with its stylishly dressed occupants. It was so very classy and grown up.

The places he had recently introduced me to were not like the teenybopper clubs I was used to going to with the cheating ex with scantily dressed women, too cool for school feminine guys, when you couldn't tell if they were straight or gay. Trust me, a girl shouldn't have to guess. I want my guy to only have eyes for me. In the club scene I was used to with the ex, guys had highly gelled spiky hair, wore tight t-shirts, bracelets, necklaces/chokers, and tight jeans. Now that I think about it, this description sounds just like my cheating ex and his too close for comfort roommate, hmm?

The new world I had stepped into was very chic and stylish and an exciting change of pace. Men wore sports coats, nice crisp button up shirts, neat and pressed jeans, and nice shiny shoes. I felt comfortable here and loved the ambiance immediately. However, being thrown into a group of his friends as well as co-workers was a bit much for our first date, so naturally I decided to call a taxi and call it a night after a few moments. He walked me out to the taxi, we hugged, and I was on my way home, feeling great.

That evening he sent a text thanking me for a lovely evening as only a gentleman would. I fell asleep blissfully happy, had sweet dreams and woke up to a very sweet email from Ajit.

Hello Pretty One,

It was nice meeting up with you. You really are beautiful. I feel like I just want to hold you, watch a movie or spend time with you. Maybe take you out to dinner again? I would love to see the photos that we took together. Have a good day.
xo
Ajit

After a day, I responded.

Hi Ajit,

Thanks so much for taking me out, I had a good time. Let's keep in touch. You seem like a really cool guy.
(I attached the photos we had taken together that night.)

Hugs & Smiles,

He responded the same day.

Hello Pretty One. (And yes, he really did refer to me as Pretty One.)

You are gorgeous. The photos look great. Well, you look great, being the model and all. I would love to see you again. You know, I did photography at some point. However, while in the process of moving, I managed to lose my camera. Anyhow, it would be great to spend time with you. Let's get together, if you want.

xo,
Ajit

I responded.

Hi Ajit,

I would love to hang out again. Call me when you want to get together. Have a beautiful day!

Hugs & Smiles,

Over the next few days he left sweet voicemails as well as sent sweet text messages throughout the day as well as calls in the morning to wish me a good morning and in the evening simply to wish me a good night. I felt happy each time I would hear from him. His voice was delightful and I absolutely adored his beautiful accent. We decided to meet up again.

This time a friend of mine was in town and staying with me, so he invited her to come along too. I thought it was sweet of him to invite my friend along. Getting in good with my best girlfriend as well was a smart move. Over drinks, they chatted more than he & I for a moment. She was always the more outgoing one of the two of us and the most outspoken one as usual. She constantly asked him questions. She's very blunt and extremely funny.

Lacey: *"What do you do for a living?"*

Ajit shyly responded: *"I am the founder of a video game company."*

Lacey asked: *"What sort of car do you drive?"*

Ajit responded: *"A black Mercedes."*

Lacey asked: *"If you ever hurt my friend, I'll kick your butt. You better treat her right."*

I smiled nervously and looked away, completely embarrassed. He smiled at me, holding my hand and pulled me closer.

I mainly exchanged sweet and shy glances with him for the remainder of the evening. Once, even veering off onto the beautiful bar, but he demanded my attention asking, "What are you looking at?" As valet so kindly returned the car, we were off to dance the evening away at a very posh, new and ultra-exclusive Hollywood hotspot, Boulevard de Amour.

We walked straight to the front of the line, flashing beyond the red velvet ropes. I was astonished and at the same time taken aback by the beauty and elegance of the venue. The waterfall was a sight to be seen and immediately looking onward to the blazing fireplace, which was so appropriately stationed in the center of the walkway as the curtained bungalows neatly aligned our journey into one of the most beautiful clubs I had ever seen. I had been to several clubs before, because of what the cheating ex did for a living, but this place was pure class in every sense of the word. The beauty of the venue was alarming.

As we stepped inside, I immediately fell in love with one room after the next. There were so many separate and glamorous rooms throughout the club. The dance floor was wide as well as long, just perfect for a grand entrance. There were beautiful velvet chairs and sofas off to the side of the dance floor. The upstairs was pure heaven in all white, so plush. I felt as though I had stepped inside someone's private mansion and having a visit, which was so very welcoming. Everything about the venue was grand. He was also a complete gentleman, which added to the excitement of the night.

The music was incredible and because of my love of dancing, he joined me on the dance floor. The music was amazing and the perfect tempo. The DJ played hit after hit and Ajit and I sure did vibe well. He was a great dancer to my surprise and I loved teasing him all night long as I playfully and flirtatiously danced alongside of him. It had turned out to be a great night and we had incredible chemistry, definitely a feeling I had never experienced before.

As we took a break from dancing on the dance floor, I noticed that we were for the first time walking hand in hand. We took photos as we perched down onto the comfy sofa which was to the side of the dance floor, so L.A. to basically have a photo shoot in front of everyone, but I enjoyed every second of it with him. The photos were so cute and the smiles on our faces revealed how happy we were together. We were sitting there talking and just holding hands and before I knew it, it was as if we were the only two in the venue, I noticed that my breathing quickened and suddenly I no longer heard the music playing, he reached over and put his hand on the side of my face and our eyes locked.

"a pretty bold move
for me, but..."

Jamaican Me Dance

{ CHAPTER FOURTEEN }

I walked back to my room, exhausted from a long evening, headed to bed and fell fast asleep. The next morning, Jessica and I met up for breakfast as usual and exchanged stories from the night before. Then we proceeded to our lounge chairs while sporting our bikinis and continued planning and plotting our evening of fun. We were both single and on vacation in Jamaica.

We were heading to the most popular club on the Island, The Forest. I was excited. I had read about this club online while searching for fun places to visit while on the island. As we were chatting, I stopped mid conversation as slowly sat up from my lounge chair, noticing a very handsome islander smiling at me as he was walking over to me. I quickly noticed that he had beautiful dark brown skin and shiny long black hair. He was very beautiful and very exotic looking, just my type. I immediately sat up, wearing my little red and white polka dot bikini, tipped up my large sunhat, slid down my sunglasses and started chatting with him. This was a pretty bold move for me, but he had caught my eye and I was not going to allow him to just pass me by. We took a photo together and I found out that he was a gorgeous mix of Indian from East India and Jamaican, pure hotness and what a combination. He was truly stunning and a delight to look at. His accent reeled me in even more. He sounded so exotic and his accent was strong, which I love, though I could barely understand what he was saying at times, because of his thick accent. However, I understood just enough and simply enjoyed the view standing before me. I told him that a few girls and I were heading to The Forest tonight and he said he would meet me there. Score!

After our quick chat, he was on his way and I decided to take a walk along the beach to look for more souvenirs. While passing by one stand, another island guy, Joe, stopped me to chat. He had colorful items at his booth. He was quite the funny guy, so I thought why not let him know about our plans of going to The Forest tonight as well. He said he would already be heading there so he would see us there. Excellent, I thought. The more the merrier. The locals were incredibly friendly and easygoing and I loved the down to earth vibe.

After dinner, Jessica & I planned to meet up in an hour to head over to The Forest. I got dressed in my cutest outfit that I had been excited to wear. I slipped into my short and sexy hot pink form fitting mini dress, which had strings that tied into a bow at the bottom on the sides. I stepped into my platform heels which made my legs appear longer than they already are, applied my shiny lip gloss, put on my large blue hoop earrings, applied minimum makeup and I was ready to go. My hair cascaded halfway down my back in long layers and moved about as I descended the cottage steps of Summer Country Cottages. Jessica looked very Upper East Side New York in her ladies who lunch respectable and demur pale blue sundress with a length just below her knees. While our styles were complete opposites, we looked hot and ready to head to the club.

The hotel manager and his wife picked us up and we were on our way. We arrived at The Forest and it was packed. There was a line of cars waiting to get in. On Thursdays, girls got into the club for free. As we were walking past the admission window, we laughed when glancing up at the sign that said "No drugs, no prostitutes and no hoodlums" amongst other rules for entering The Forest. We had clearly made the cut with flying colors. The place looked so pretty. Once we stepped inside, we got to see what an enormous place it really was and the forest themed painted walls were creative and colorful. We headed upstairs where the crowd was dancing and mingling while dancehall music played. We joined in by dancing a bit to the music and then headed to the bar for drinks.

When to my surprise, Island Boy had arrived alongside me and greeted me with a warm smile and a big hug. He immediately ordered me a drink as we chatted at the bar. He seemed amazed by my outfit as well as by my appearance. He couldn't seem to keep his eyes off me. I was delighted. He kept his eyes on me all night long.

I introduced him to my newfound Jamaican friends and one New Yorker and he fit right in. He even waited for me right by the door whenever I headed to the powder room to freshen up and brush my hair. He navigated me through the crowd as we walked hand in hand, which I appreciated greatly and didn't mind at all as the club was nearly packed to capacity, which was at times hard to walk through. We had a drink and immediately went downstairs to V.I.P. We danced the night away. We stood and observed extremely lively dancers dancing in a very provocative manner all the way down to the floor surrounding us at every angle around the club. The dancehall music had a really cool vibe and quite frankly, the music moved me. While we danced close, he respected my space boundaries and just how low he could go with me on the dance floor. There was a nice vibe going on between us and the moment was temporarily interrupted when the guy I had met on the beach came over to say hello.

There was some sort of chemistry brewing up between us as we continued dancing all night long. Amidst the lively dancers winding and grinding all around us, he managed to keep our dancing together sexy and respectful, which I enjoyed immensely. When the night started to wind down, we went for a walk outside of the club for a bit of fresh air.

"... crawling up and against
the walls and across ...

Models' Night Out

{ CHAPTER FIFTEEN }

It was another Girls' Night Out. My girlfriends and I always celebrated each other birthdays with dinner and karaoke. My girlfriends and I are totally supportive of each other and a birthday was always a cause for celebration. While we all lived fairly close, because of our busy lives which consisted of modeling, boys, dining out, traveling, acting, and singing, always an adventure, we were delighted when girls night came around, because we would finally make time to see each other.

I was completely excited to see my girls, but somehow the day had dragged along. It was a bit chilly outside and the comfort of my own home felt ideal. However, never one to let my girls down, I immediately got myself into the going out mode. I quickly ran over to my laptop, clicked onto the iTunes button, selected internet radio, Bollywood tunes was my music of choice, as beats and melodies blared and were music to my ears, which immediately put me into a festive mood!

I headed to my bathroom, stepped into the shower and allowed the warm water to splash against my body as scents of Laura Mercier almond coconut body wash filled the air as I lathered my body. Immediately after my shower, I sprayed a spritz of fresh pineapple and coconut all over my body, drying off and quickly applied Palmer's coco butter all over myself. The combination of scents smelled amazing and I felt as fresh as can be.

Then I was off to make decisions on my wardrobe. My closet is filled with only clothes, which I love, since I edit my closet each month and send some items off to donate to charity. I was faced with a dilemma, which mood was I in tonight? As I looked over my choices of numerous dresses and jeans, I knew that I wanted to be warm. What's a girl to wear tonight? A dress, of course, but which one?

Shoes were my next decision or shall I say heels, since they are the only type of shoes I wear. For some reason flat shoes are just not me and if you know me, I just always have to be me, no matter what. I decided on a dress, which was a pretty blue mini dress. I slipped into my shiny patent leather, four and a half inch red heels, which were just screaming to be worn. They were both sexy and fierce at once and just waiting to be taken for a night out on the town. As I was slipping into my heels, the phone rang. The hot Australian reporter wanted to know exactly where we were heading so he could meet up and film us at the birthday celebration. Only in Hollywood, right? However, he seemed alarmed when I told him I was headed to the location and the amount it would cost from my place in a cab. I called for a cab and just as I was putting my last few items into my handbag, the call from the cab company alerted me that my cab had arrived. I gathered my handbag, a light jacket to shield me from the brisk weather, my two pink Victoria's Secret gift bags for the birthday girls and I was on my way.

Into the cab I went and arrived fifteen minutes past seven o'clock, because while I do love the girls, they are always notoriously late. I tipped the cab driver, surprised that it only cost ten dollars instead of the seventeen dollars the cab company had quoted me over the phone. I headed inside of the Korean BBQ. I was hoping to make a grand entrance, but to my surprise, when I told the hostess my name, I realized that I was still the first one to arrive from our party.

As I sat patiently for ten minutes underneath the heat lamps, keeping warm, thank goodness, birthday girl number one had arrived, Claudia. We embraced and I immediately gave her my gift, My Desire is was it was called, in body wash, moisturizer as well as spray from Victoria's Secret, the name so fitting for her. She always drives the boys wild with her smile and exotic looks. While she looks like a curvaceous pin-up model with jet black hair and signature red lips, you would never guess that her super power was that she could rap on cue. Claudia and I had met on a photo shoot in Thailand. We were both modeling for a bikini calendar and became fast friends. Claudia and I headed over to our reserved table and chatted a bit when suddenly girl number two showed up, Anastasia.

Anastasia is adorable as always with her beautiful long, layered locks, wearing her bright pink top underneath her black fitted vest and super cute skinny jeans and high heels. Anastasia is a blonde bombshell who is famously known to showcase her fabulous hair, turning her head in slow motion in highly recognized hair commercials. I bet you would be surprised to know that she is known to breakdance at the drop of a hat. Anastasia had a purple stylish gift bags in hand. Claudia had introduced me to Anastasia on a photo shoot we all did together as models in Turks & Caicos. Anastasia was the strong, very opinionated one with the wits and smarts of someone older, however she was the youngest of all of us. Imagine that. As for me, my long legs and bikini clad body has been known to grace numerous swimsuit calendars and my mega watt smile has lit up a number of print ads and billboards. I'm also known to sing such high notes that could easily shatter glass, totally pitch perfect.

As you can see, we're a force to reckon with. Don't be quick to judge a book solely by it's cover, as you may be surprised at what lies within.

We all embraced and before you know it, birthday girl number two had arrived, a girl I had not met before. Her name was Racquel. She had long silky black waist-length hair with blue streaks in it and a tiny frame, which fit perfectly into her purple bodycon dress and laced up thigh high black boots. She was very exotic looking and had arrived with a surprise, she had brought along a guy to our All Girls' Night Out. No worries. He was welcome to join us since he was already here, we found it rather odd for her to invite him. I was told that she's always the wild card, completely fun, rowdy and always full of surprises. Claudia told me that Racquel's behavior on occasions seemed to be questionable, but underneath it all, she was a girl with a heart of gold. After all, every girl was once a diamond in the rough at some point waiting for a chance to shine like the gem they were always meant to be. Besides I'm sure that under our influence, her personal super power will reveal itself soon enough, it just takes time.

We decided on the all-you-can-eat dish. After all, we were at a Korean BBQ, which displayed a grill at the center of our table. Being the non-domestic divas that we are, Claudia and I declined the offer to cook, while Anastasia and Racquel were delighted to, being the domestic divas that they are, which worked out perfectly. Although I'm not a huge meat eater, I must admit that the large pieces of meat, which arrived at our table was absolutely delicious once cooked and cut into tiny thin slices. We ate plenty, because the food was so tasty. However, the smaller side dishes were not my favorite. The flavors were not in sync with what I had in mind. Although I'm always excited to try something knew, kimchi was also not agreeing with my palette.

We had a blast dining; gossiping as only girls do, taking group photos at dinner as models do, and some of us were getting drunk as a particular new girl was doing at the moment. Raquel could not seem to hold her liquor. Racquel had one soju too many. Poor intoxicated girl, but as adorable as ever. She was simply being herself, in all of her fun glory, which we all loved and continued laughing with her the entire time, because she was pure entertainment. Perhaps she was just nervous to be hanging out with us for the first time and lost count of how many drinks she had downed.

After paying the bill, valet gathered our cars and we were off to our usual karaoke spot. Okay, after making a quick stop at PinkBerry, a simply scrumptious fruity Korean yogurt shop. My yogurt included three toppings: almonds, bananas, and kiwi, yummy. I'm always one to get excited about dessert and the yogurt totally hit the spot.

Girl number four had arrived, Amber, just in time to stuff us all into her Audi. We left Claudia's boyfriend's car, the luxury beamer, around the corner parked. We were flying through the streets of Koreatown in Claudia's ex's shiny new BMW blasting rap songs, singing and dancing with the windows down. In the midst of all of this, we were talking about boys and dating. What fun! I was enjoying the night out with my girls. It felt like we were in high school again or better yet at University, borrowing the car from our parents and staying out to wee hours of the night, but sure to make it home in time for curfew.

We arrived at our karaoke spot, booked our private room, and singing was now in full swing. The girls started out singing slow ballots to warm up or maybe they were just in more of a romantic mood. However, Amber and I flipped the script with more fast-paced songs, Dontcha' by The Pussycat Dolls, which had everyone dancing, singing, and up out of their seats. The new girl, Racquel, was so intoxicated that she began crawling up and against the walls and across the tables and once again the photo shoots were in full swing. We even shot video of this little wild night, so much fun!

As midnight approached, we realized that some of us had long journeys home and ended the evening, once again, we all piled into Amber's car. We dropped everyone off at Claudia's ex's BMW and Amber and I hugged each other goodbye as I finally made it back home. While the night had started off slow, it was in full swing and had turned out to be so much fun. I must say, I cannot wait until our next Girls' Night Out. As always, it's guaranteed to be a blast.

"I opened the doors and was at once intoxicated..."

Island Vibe

{ CHAPTER SIXTEEN }

From the moment I stepped off the plane, I knew I had made the right choice. I was in paradise at last. Ahhhh... complete sunshine on the Caribbean island of Jamaica. My driver was waiting for me with the warmest smile, which spread cheerfully across his face. He was holding a sign, which read "Summer Country," the name of the cottages I would be staying at. We greeted each other and were on our way.

An hour and thirty-minute drive took less than an hour. My driver, Ernie, knew how to navigate the road, which was filled with beautiful colorful Barbie-Doll looking homes, hoards of people walking alongside the roads, goats sprinkled the streets and just a brand new atmosphere, which was exactly what I needed. As we were passing through the city, there were fruit vendors everywhere and Bernie asked if I wanted sugar cane. I had never had sugar cane, so he pulled over immediately and bought me a bag full. The sugar cane was absolutely mouthwatering delicious. I was immediately in love with this sugary delicious stalk, which flowed of sweet juices. We chatted along the way and very quickly reached our destination "Summer Country."

A very welcoming staff immediately greeted me as I checked in. Everyone was so friendly and happy to see me and I was overjoyed by their kindness. I was escorted through a beautiful jungle of colorful two storied cottages as we headed towards the beach. There were beautiful palm trees all around me. There was a pretty stone statue of a Rasta man with an ivory and tan color face with dreads who looked pleasantly mellow. There was a Zen area, which had a wooden bench, surrounded by even more palm trees, which read from a cement plate on the ground "You Are Here!" I thought to myself "Yes, I am, I have arrived in paradise at last." The weather was perfect at about 90 degrees or more with 100 percent humidity and Summer Country was like an amazing and tropical play land.

I tipped the bellman after he ushered me into my colorful cottage. I opened the doors and was at once intoxicated by all of the beautiful colors, which surrounded me. My bed was yellow, the lamp was turquoise, the rug was lime green, and the walls were peach. Every new color fascinated me. The cottage was so pretty and lively with color, and I loved it. I couldn't believe I was finally in Jamaica. I changed out of my travel clothes: cute low-waist jeans and a tiny coral top covered up by a small jacket. I showered, put on my favorite purple, tie-dye floor-length dress and walked through the sand and stepped into the beachfront restaurant.

The tables were colorfully decorated with vibrant yellow, pink, orange, and turquoise as couples sat and dined. I felt just fine as a single. I dined on a deliciously festive plate of pasta with chicken and veggies alongside the coconut shrimp appetizer, which was just scrumptious. Both were extremely delicious and so full of flavor. I chatted with the female waiters a bit and one waiter asked if I wanted company, because there was a girl at another table who was staying at the cottages as well, traveling solo. I declined and said that I was fine. It just felt really nice sitting there enjoying the view and having my meal alone in silence, enjoying every single bite on my very first night on the island. I needed a moment to myself. After dinner, I walked along the beach. It was a bit dark but I wanted to have a look around. I headed off to bed with a smile. My first night in paradise, excited to see what the next day would bring.

I headed to breakfast the next morning and was immediately amazed by the bright sun and the picturesque view before me. The girl who was also staying at the cottage and traveling solo walked over to my table and introduced herself. We decided to have breakfast together and each day after that. She was so cool and fun and we had so much in common. We chatted about cute boys, traveling, shopping, our love of the DVD and book The Secret, and other fun girl stuff. We met up on the beach and lounged in the beach chairs in our teeny bikinis as we attracted boys left and right, mainly locals from all over the island. It was a fun experience and just what I imagined my trip to Jamaica to be. Security stood close by to make sure the Island boys and vendors were of our liking and not interrupting our girl chat. We ordered Jamaican chicken patties, sweet tropical juices, and plenty of fruit and sugar cane as we layed out on the beach. We didn't have to get up and to go anywhere for food and drinks, because vendors were constantly coming up to us and offering us goodies as we relaxed. Oh, the laid back Island life, I love it!

Shantelle!

ABOUT THE AUTHOR

Shantelle is the author of *Confessions of an Internet Model: How I Succeeded on the World Wide Web, Jet Set Dreams: A Girl's Guide to Flying High* & contributed to the anthology *Open Doors: Fractured Fairy Tales.* Shantelle enjoys traveling the world & living by the beach in sunny Southern California as she's a true beach lover.

Visit her website at: www.**Shantelle**.net

Shantelle!

www.ingramcontent.com/pod-product-compliance
Lightning Source LLC
Chambersburg PA
CBHW072009170626
46813CB00005B/2076